Witches and Warriors

Legends from the Shropshire Marches

Retold by Karen Lowe
Illustrated by Robin Lawrie

Reprinted 1995 and 2002
ISBN 0-903802-46-5 © Text: Karen Lowe
                         © Illustrations: Robin Lawrie
Book Design: Sarah Barker
Editing: Helen Sample
Published by Shropshire Books, The Publishing Division of Shropshire County
Leisure Services in association with Wheaton Publishers Ltd.
Printed in Great Britain by Livesey Ltd., Shrewsbury.

In Memory of my father,
Gordon William Jones, a 'Shropshire lad'

Contents

Acknowledgements

Towards the end of the last century, many of the customs and folktales of the Shropshire area were collected by Georgina Jackson. Her book, "Shropshire Folklore", edited by Charlotte Burne, was published in 1883. Some of these tales are retold in this collection.

The traditional Welsh borderland rhyme, 'Nicky Nicky Nye', appears in a collection by Ruth Tongue, "Forgotten Folk Tales of the English Counties", published by Routledge in 1971, and is reprinted here with their kind permission.

Fulk FitzWarin's adventures originally appeared as an Anglo-Norman story that blended together history, local legend and Arthurian romance. It was translated in 1904 by Alice Kemp-Welch in "The History of Fulk Fitz-Warine".

The exploits of the knights of the Round Table at Hawkstone were based on traditional folk tales and written down by Jane Hill in "The Antiquities of Hawkstone", published in 1834.

The Author

Born in Gower, South Wales, Karen moved to Shrewsbury when she was five. Her story-writing career began at Featherbed Lane Junior School, where she wrote novels about ponies and plays about princesses. She survived the bleak and windswept corridors of the Priory Grammar School for Girls to study French, German and English for a B.A. degree in London, and spent the following five years working her way round the Monopoly board of London as a secretary - in Fleet Street, Piccadilly, Mayfair, Strand...
In 1979 she returned to Shrewsbury where she lives with husband, two children and two guinea pigs called Pippin and Squeak. She now works as a secretary with Shropshire Libraries.

For some years she wrote historical romances and short stories for grown-ups, which won prizes on London's "Capital Radio" and more recently at Shropshire's Minsterley Eisteddfod. Through her involvement with the Gateway Writers' Circle she has helped produce two collections of the Group's short stories and poems, published in aid of local charities. Her stories for children have featured on BBC TV's Playschool while others were accepted for Radio 4's "Listening Corner" and "Cat's Whiskers". An 'early reader' story is due for publication next year.

The Illustrator

Robin Lawrie was born into a coal mining family in Scotland. He spent his early years in the mining village of Lesmahagow, Lanarkshire.

In 1953 he went to live in Canada with his parents but returned to Britain in 1968 to work as a freelance illustrator. He has illustrated about eighty books for children and has written and illustrated another five.

For thirteen years Robin lived and worked in London but he now lives in Shropshire with his wife and two children aged 8 and 6 in a 300 year old farmhouse between Earls Hill and the Stiperstones. He spends his spare time restoring his house, painting portraits and pursuing his interest in vintage cars and local history.

Introduction

Once upon a time...

Until the middle of the last century, people rarely travelled far
beyond their own villages. They spent their whole lives amongst
the same fields, farms and cottages. They had no TV or radio to
entertain them or bring them news. They could not afford books,
and indeed few could even read. People had yet to discover
what caused illnesses or how to cure them. They knew little
about the way the Earth was shaped over millions of years. They
tried to understand and explain the world around them through
the stories they told. Often, the pools or trees where they lived
would remind them of stories about their families and friends.

They enjoyed listening to stories, and entertained each other
with tales they had heard of adventures in far-off lands. How
hard it must have been for them to imagine an ocean when they
had never seen the sea, or to picture strange beasts like elephants,
giraffes or kangaroos.

There were tales too of heroes and battles closer to home. In
the days of the Romans there had been battles with the Celts in
their hilltop forts, twenty-five of which can still be traced in
Shropshire. Then in 1066 William and his Norman armies
invaded England, driving the Welsh back into the hills. He built a
string of castles along the borderland between England and Wales,
where he set up his best knights as Lords of the March, to keep
the Welsh out and subdue English rebellion.

The ruins of these castles still remain, and with them, the
wealth of stories, told and retold down the ages, which are our
Marcher heritage.

Witches
and
Ghosts

Jenny Greenteeth

Shropshire children were always
warned not to play near ponds, for under
the weeds of the stagnant water there
lived a witch.
Stray too close to the water's edge and
the old woman might reach out her long bony
arms and drag you in.

Don't stray too near to the water, my dears,
Where the weed's thick pillow
Stifles the water. Beware!
Don't stand too close to the edge, my dears,
Where long fingers reach,
And bony arms sneak. Beware!
Don't gaze too long in the water, my dears.
See her laughter bubble!
See her tangled hair! Who's there?
Jenny Greenteeth!

3

Nicky Nicky Nye

Just across the border in Wales, there was an ogre who lived in the rivers. He lay in wait to snatch unwary children who played too close to the riverbank. His eyes were hideous and green and his name was Nicky Nicky Nye. Children learned a rhyme to remind themselves of the danger of playing by the water:

Nicky Nicky Nye
He pulls you down
Underneath the water
To drown, drown, die..

The Mermaid of Child's Ercall

Early one morning, two men set off to work on a farm near Child's Ercall. As they made their way as usual across the fields towards the horsepond, they saw something in the water, basking like a seal in the sun.

At first the men were frightened for it was no ordinary creature. As they drew nearer, they saw it wasn't an animal at all but a beautiful mermaid.

"Tis the work of witchcraft," they said, and feared she would spirit them away.
But the mermaid spoke gently to them and soon they forgot their fears. As they listened to her voice, they fell in love with her.

"There's much treasure hidden beneath the water," the mermaid told them. "I will share it with you."

The two men looked doubtful, but the mermaid's sweet voice persuaded them.

"I will give you all the gold you can carry," she said. "But you must come to me in the water and take it from me."
The men nodded and started towards her. Deeper and deeper into the cold water they waded to where the mermaid sat. When they were up to their chins, the mermaid gave a flick of her fishy tail and dived to the bottom of the pond. When she surfaced, she held out a lump of gold as big as a man's head.

The two men stared in wonder at the gold. Just as the mermaid had told them, they reached out and took the gold from her. Then they laughed in delight.

"If this isn't a bit of luck!" cried one of the men out loud.

At the sound of his harsh voice, the mermaid screamed. She snatched back the gold, and dived beneath the water and they never saw her again.

5

The Cobbler and the Giant

In Wales there lived a giant who had a grudge against the people of Shrewsbury. One day he decided he would be rid of them all. He dug a spadeful of earth and set off across the mountains.

"If I dump this load of earth into the Severn," he thought, "It will dam the river and the town will be flooded and its people drowned!"

He walked for some time with his heavy load, but he was not sure of the way. On and on he walked, getting tired and hot, until he reached Wellington and there he rested.

Along the road from Shrewsbury came a cobbler. He was carrying a sack full of boots and shoes he was taking home to mend for his customers in Shrewsbury.

6

When the giant saw him, he called out to him,
"Can you tell me the way to Shrewsbury?"
The cobbler looked up at the giant and trembled.
"Why do you want to know?" he asked.
"Because I'm going to dam the river with this spadeful of earth
and drown the whole town!" bellowed the giant. "Is it much
further?"

The cobbler was horrified. Drown all the people in Shrewsbury?
He'd lose all his customers! Then the cobbler gave a sly smile.
He shook his head and looked up at the giant again.
"Shrewsbury you say? Well, you'll not get there today, nor
tomorrow either. Look," and he swung the sack from his shoulder
and showed it to the giant. "I've come from Shrewsbury myself,
and I've worn out all these boots and shoes on the way."
The giant groaned. He was very tired.
"In that case, I'll go back home," he said, and he dumped the
load of earth by the road and scraped his boots clean on the
spade, and set off back to Wales.

And that is how the Wrekin came to be made out of a giant
spadeful of earth, and the smaller hill beside it, the Ercall, is where
the giant cleaned off his boots.

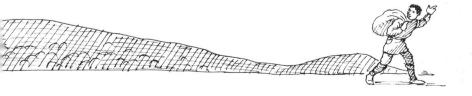

7

The Evil Eye

Long ago, at Child's Ercall, there lived a farmer who was well known and feared for his magic powers. It was said he had the Evil Eye. It gave him power over people and animals. If anyone annoyed him, all he had to do was stare at them and he could send them off in the opposite direction to the one they wanted to go. He had gained his powers, people said, by wrestling with the Devil. At night, his neighbours would hear scuffling in the lanes and the sounds of a mighty struggle. Soon afterwards they would be sure to see the farmer returning home with his clothes in disorder, just as if he had been wrestling, though they never did see the Devil.

One day, the farmer was sitting in the inn with a tankard of ale in front of him. In came a group of morris dancers to perform for the crowd. After their dancing, the men were hot and thirsty. One of them snatched up the ale from the farmer's table and swigged it down. The farmer said nothing, but stared very hard at the young man.

When the dancers left the inn to go home, the young man went with them. But they had hardly left the yard when the young man stopped.

"Come on. Hurry up. What are you waiting for?" his friends called to him. The young man tried to follow them but could not walk a step.

"I can't move!" he told them.

His friends thought he was joking. They laughed and went on their way, thinking he would soon come after them. But, try as he might, the young man could not move.

At last he could take a small step - backwards. Step by step he found himself returning to the inn where the farmer was waiting.

"That will teach you to drink my ale," the farmer told him, and to punish him, he did not let him move again until morning.

The Witch's Cave

In the days when doctors knew little about diseases and how to treat them, people blamed witches and their evil magic if they were ill. They said they had been cursed. They hung up special charms like horseshoes and silver to keep away evil spirits. In the seventeenth century, if someone was accused of being a witch, they had to prove their innocence in harsh ordeals. One ordeal was the ducking stool. This was a long beam with a stool tied to one end, a bit like a see-saw. It was set up over a pond. The woman was tied to the stool and plunged into the water. If she drowned, the court said she wasn't a witch at all for God had taken her. If she lived, then the Devil had saved her life, proving she was a witch. An old ducking stool stands in the Priory at Leominster, and models of it are to be found in Leominster Museum.

Animals were thought to be able to recognise witches and evil spirits before humans could. At night, witches rode any horse whose stable was not protected by lucky charms. In the morning, the owner would find the horse exhausted. They called it 'hag-ridden'.

The red sandstone hills around Bridgnorth are riddled with caves where people lived until early this century. In the cliffs at the top of Hermitage Hill is a cave named after a hermit who lived there in Saxon times. The cave once had three chambers and a chapel downstairs and an upper room. These have weathered and crumbled away over the years, but the arched roof and the shape of the lower rooms and staircase can still be seen. The cave beside it later became famous for quite a different person. It is called the Witch's Cave. The witch who once lived there is said to have had the power to stop horses in their tracks. Since the hill below the cave is steep, it is perhaps not surprising that horses pulling heavy carts up the road would come to a halt. People said that the old witch used to fly out from her cave every night on her broomstick to go about her evil work.

In the cliffs opposite lived another witch who had the power to change herself into a cat or a hare. When she changed into a hare, she would set off across the meadows beside the river. All the town's dogs would chase hard after her, but never once did they catch her.

The Devil's Chair

On the Stiperstones there is a ragged peak of rocks known as the Devil's Chair. This rock is very hard quartzite, formed from the molten magma beneath the earth's crust millions of years ago. With time, the softer rock that used to cover it has been weathered away, leaving the crest of rocks like the spine of a dinosaur.

The Devil is said to sit on this rocky throne to survey his kingdom. On the longest night of the year, he would summon his court together. All the witches and evil spirits who lived in the Marches met to choose their king for the year.

According to the legend, the rocks of the Devil's Chair were brought there by the Devil. He was on his way from Ireland with his apron full of stones. He was going to fill in the valley on the hillside, known as Hell's Gutter. But it was heavy work and the day was hot. He soon grew tired crossing the hills with his load, and sat down on the highest rock of the Stiperstones to rest. As he stood up again, his apronstrings broke, and the rocks tumbled out. The Devil cursed them and left them where they lay, scattered over the hillside. People say that, when the weather is hot, you can smell the brimstone on them.

Mitchell's Fold

On Stapeley Hill there is a circle of boulders, set out like the numbers on a clock-face. The place is known as Mitchell's Fold, and the stones were put there 4,000 years ago by the people of the Bronze Age. Perhaps the stone circle was a place of worship; perhaps it was a calendar to help them map the moon and stars. But there is a legend which gives quite a different reason for the stone circle.

Once there was a great drought in the country. The wells dried up, the crops failed, and the animals were dying. The people were near to starving when a good witch took pity on them. She sent a magic cow which was kept on Stapeley Hill. This cow would produce milk enough for everyone who came to her, provided they took only one bucket each to be filled.

An evil witch was jealous of the good witch's powers and decided to spite her. At midnight, she took a sieve and went to milk the cow. The cow gave enough milk to fill a bucket many times over, but still the witch went on milking. The cow was puzzled by this, then a great storm broke. As the lightning flashed, the cow saw the great pool of wasted milk that had run through the sieve, and realised she had been tricked. In fury she kicked out at the witch and set off down the hill at a gallop, never to be seen again.

Next morning, when the people brought their buckets to milk the cow, they were upset to find the beast had gone. They saw the sieve and the wasted milk and guessed what had happened.

As for the bad witch, she had been turned to stone as her punishment. The people set a ring of stones around her to make sure she would never escape and do evil again.

You can see the story of the marvellous milch cow carved around a sandstone pillar in Middleton Church near Stapeley Hill. The carvings were made in 1879 by the vicar at that time, Reverend Brewster.

The Ghostly Hand

A young woman once lived with her aunt who was bad-tempered and spiteful. Nothing the niece did pleased her aunt. The old woman always stopped her going out and enjoying herself.

Then the old aunt decided she would go and live in Paris, but she did not ask her niece to go with her. Instead the young woman was sent to live with friends at Bridgnorth. The niece was pleased, for she was glad to be among friends.

One morning, her friends decided to visit relatives at Cleobury North and took the niece with them. They set off in their carriage, but they hadn't travelled far before the horse came to a sudden halt.

"Get on with you!" the coachman shouted and cracked his whip, but the horse did not move. He whipped the horse harder but still the animal refused to go any further. As the coachman raised his whip again, the niece took pity on the horse and cried out to stop him.

"Let me try!" she said, for she had been brought up in the country and was used to animals. She got down from the coach and talked gently to the horse to reassure it. She could see the horse was terrified of something. Its eyes rolled white and it was trembling. She took hold of its bridle and tried to lead the horse forward as she gently tapped its back with the whip.

At once, she found herself thrown back against the fence as if some great force had pushed her. She felt suddenly afraid. She could see nothing in the road, and yet she felt something close by her that stopped her moving.

Then slowly the fingertips, the wrist and arm of gigantic size appeared before her. The hand was holding the horse fast by its neck. Just then, across the fields, she heard the chime of the church clock at Bridgnorth; it was midday. The hand loosed its grip and vanished from sight.

They went on their way as best they could, for the horse was still frightened, and it was never fit to pull the carriage again.

Some days later news reached the niece that her aunt had been taken ill and had died in Paris, shortly before noon on the day of that journey.

The White Lady of Longnor

By the Leebotwood road, there was a pond called the Black Pool. It was said to be bottomless, and it was haunted by the ghost of a young woman known as the White Lady.

The young woman was engaged to be married, but the man she loved left her and married someone else. Broken-hearted, she threw herself into the pool and was drowned. Sometimes at night her ghost emerged from the pool, dressed in white like a bride.

One evening, there was a party at the Villa nearby. There was ale in plenty and a fiddler called Joe Wigley played for the people to dance. A beautiful young woman came and joined in their dances, dressed in a white silk gown. As they danced round and round in a large circle, the woman danced with them. No-one knew her name, but she was so light and graceful that many a young man wanted her for his partner. They tried to catch hold of her hand, but somehow they couldn't touch her.

As the night wore on and the dawn began to break, the young woman disappeared. The dancers searched for her. Wherever had she gone? It was only then they realised she was the White Lady. At that, they were all so terrified to think they had danced with a ghost, that no-one ever danced at the Villa again.

The Bagbury Bull

At Bagbury Farm on the Welsh border, there once lived a mean and bad-tempered squire. He paid his farmworkers poorly, and ill-treated them. After his death, his soul could not rest because of the wicked life he had led. Late at night, his ghost took on the shape of a bull and appeared in the farm buildings. There he would bellow until the boards and tiles flew off the barns. That was bad enough for his neighbours who had to put up with the noise, but he began to appear earlier in the evening and the noise went on for hours. It was too much to bear so they called in twelve parsons to lay his spirit to rest.

The parsons came to the farm and read from the Bible, to try to quieten the raging bull, but the squire's spirit was too strong and angry for them. At last the parsons managed to coax the ghostly bull into the church at Hyssington. Each of them carried a lighted candle, for it was well known that a ghost has no power by light. One of the parsons, a wise old man who was blind, knew very well what the bull got up to, and carried his candle hidden in his top-boot.

Into the church they went. At once the bull gave a mighty bellow and rushed at them. The fierce gust of wind as he passed put out all their candles: all, that is except one. The blind parson still had his candle in his boot.

"Come and light your candles by mine," he told the others.

But in that moment's darkness, the squire's powers increased. The bull grew and grew, until its vast bulk cracked the church walls.

As quickly as they could, the parsons lit their candles again and hurriedly began to read from the Bible. For hours they read, until at length the power of the squire began to weaken once more. Smaller and smaller his ghost grew until at last they could catch him inside a snuffbox.

"Lay me under Bagbury Bridge," said the squire's ghost, but the parsons refused, knowing full well he would try to cause more trouble. Instead he was sent away to be buried in the Red Sea.

But people remembered the fearsome power of the squire's ghost, and they were afraid to cross the bridge. They were sure his spirit haunted it. When they reached the bridge, they got down from their horses and led them across as quietly as they could, afraid the evil spirit might hear them and come after them.

Some people think the squire's ghost was buried under the stone at the church door. If that stone were ever loosened, the bull would appear again, only more powerful than before.

Blount's Pool

In Kinlet Church is the tomb of the last squire of Kinlet, Sir George Blount, who died in 1581. The Elizabethan monument shows the stone figures of the squire and his wife kneeling with their son and daughter. Under the monument is said to be a small bottle containing the Squire's ghost. If ever the bottle is broken, his spirit will come back to haunt Kinlet Hall again.

The squire's son died young, but his daughter Dorothy lived to defy him. Much to her father's anger, she fell in love with their page-boy. She refused to choose any other husband, and the squire would not let her marry the page. But the page loved her, and every time a gentleman came to the Hall to visit her, the page would tell him she was not at home.

When the squire died, the daughter inherited all his money and lands. At last she was free to marry the page she had always loved. But they did not live happily ever after.

Soon after their wedding, the squire's spirit returned, furious that she had disobeyed him. When the family were seated at dinner, his ghost would appear, driving his coach and four white horses across the dinner table.

His ghost was said to live nearby in Blount's Pool. Sometimes when the village women took their washing there, the squire's hideous ghost would come riding out of the water at them and frighten them away.

Long after the Hall had been left empty, the cellars were said to be full of wine and ale barrels. No-one dared to steal them for fear of angering Squire Kinlet's ghost.

Madam Pigott's Armchair

The land around Chetwynd and Edgmond is haunted by the dreadful ghost of Madam Pigott. Her family had held the land and house at Chetwynd for generations. Her husband was a cruel man who cared little about her. All he wanted was a son to inherit the estate. When her child was about to be born, the doctor warned him that Madam Pigott's life was in danger. If he tried to save her, he would probably lose the child. He could not save them both. The squire made up his mind.

"The root must be lopped to save the branch," he told the doctor, for his wife's life meant nothing to him.

The doctor was shocked at the Squire's words. He did his best to save both Madam Piggot and the child, but despite all his efforts, she and her baby died. The squire felt no grief for her. Madam Piggot was so outraged at the way her husband had treated her that her spirit could not rest.

Every night at midnight her ghost came from the old Rectory to wander the fields and lanes around Edgmond.

On a moonlit night she could be seen on Cheney Hill where the lane is dark and the hedges high. People renamed it Madam Pigott's Hill. Near the top was a gnarled old tree. It was called Madam Pigott's Armchair, for here her ghost would sit with her baby in her arms, combing the child's hair.

If anyone rode by after dark, she and her black cat would jump up on the horse's back. She would cling fast to the rider with her demonic strength. Nothing the rider could do would shake her free, no matter how hard he twisted and turned. Only when he reached water would she loosen her hold, for ghosts cannot cross water.

Haunted by his wife's ghost and his guilty conscience, the squire shut up the house and went to live abroad. When Madam Pigott's relatives came to mind the empty house, their young daughter said that often on a moonlit night she looked out of her window and saw a pale white figure wandering sadly in the garden.

Warriors
and
Knights

Sir Humphrey Kynaston
~ Highwayman ~

In Elizabethan times, the wool merchants of Shrewsbury used to buy Welsh cloth at Oswestry market and bring it back to Shrewsbury to be made up. The cloth was then sent to London to be sold abroad. As they grew wealthy, the merchants built themselves fine timber houses. Some, like Owens, Irelands, and Rowleys Mansions, are still to be seen in Shrewsbury. But that journey to market to buy cloth was dangerous, for their saddlebags were full of silver and gold, and on the roads the highwaymen were waiting.

At Nesscliffe, the road from Shrewsbury lies in the shadow of a wooded hill. On the hilltop, the highwaymen lay in wait, watching the road for the merchants' horses. The old 'Wolf's Head Inn' nearby was known as a meeting place for thieves and highwaymen right up until late in the eighteenth century. So great was the risk of robbery that in 1583, the Drapers Company, to which the merchants belonged, ordered that no-one was to set out for the Monday market at Oswestry before six o'clock in the morning, or they would face a fine of six shillings and eightpence, and that they must be armed and never travel alone.

Most famous of the highwaymen is Sir Humphrey Kynaston. His family once kept the castle at Myddle, but when Kynaston inherited it, his wild living soon ran up large debts. With no money, and outlawed for his debts, Kynaston let the castle go to ruin and found himself a new home in a cave at Nesscliffe.

The cave can still be visited today, carved out of the red sandstone of the quarry. It is reached by a steep and narrow flight of steps cut in the rock. There are two small rooms divided by a pillar of rock. Carved into the rock are the initials "H.K." and the date 1564. Here Kynaston lived with his horse, and escaped all attempts by the sheriff and his men to capture him.

Kynaston's horse was no ordinary animal. By day it grazed freely in the meadows nearby and when Kynaston whistled, it would come to him at a gallop. Kynaston had its shoes put on backwards so that if anyone tried to follow the track of its hoofprints, they would be led the opposite way. At night, the horse climbed the cave steps to its stable in the outer room.

One day, Kynaston rode into the yard of Aston Hall and called for a drink. The servant brought him a silver tankard of ale. Kynaston took the ale and thanked him, but did not dismount. The servant recognised Kynaston as an outlaw and secretly gave the alarm. While Kynaston calmly drank his ale, the household planned to capture him. They closed the gates of the courtyard and stood ready to jump on him. Kynaston finished his ale. When he saw the trap they had set up, he turned his horse about. He slipped the silver tankard into his pocket and set his horse at the group of men. The horse sprang forward. In a bound it cleared both the men and the gates, and Kynaston was free.

Kynaston lived by stealing from the wealthy who travelled the high road, but he was a man with a sense of justice. Much of what he stole he gave to the poor people who lived nearby. In return, they protected him and took him food and hay for his horse. It is said that if he ever met two carts out on the road and one had three horses pulling it and the other only one, he would take the lead horse of the three and give it to the other cart, to make them even.

Many a time Kynaston outwitted the sheriff's attempts to capture him. Once, his horse is said to have jumped from the top of Nesscliffe and landed at Ellesmere, nine miles away. People said he had the Devil's help to do it. Some even said that his horse was the Devil himself. The horse is said to have jumped the river Severn at a spot where it is forty feet wide, called 'Kynaston's Leap', where, legend says, the horse's hoofprints are to be seen.

The horse's most famous jump was at Montford Bridge. There the sheriff and his men had set an ambush for Kynaston on the old stone and wooden bridge. They took up many of the planks and left a gaping hole, certain that no horse could jump it, then Kynaston could be arrested. As Kynaston rode up to the bridge, the men jumped from hiding to arrest him. But he did not stop. He set his spurs to his horse. The horse soared into the air and cleared both the men and the gaping hole in the bridge. He landed safely and escaped again.

Once more the sheriff was outwitted. Sir Humphrey Kynaston lived a free man till the end of his days in the cave at Nesscliffe. His seat, carved out of sandstone, was taken from the cave and is now part of the fireplace at the Old Three Pigeons Inn in Nesscliffe.

Ippikin, the Robber Knight

The cliffs of Wenlock Edge, between Presthope and Lutwyche Hall, are famous for a robber knight called Ippikin. Above Upper Hill Farm there is a large rock jutting out from the cliff face, which is known as Ippikin's Rock. Ippikin and his men were said to have lived in a cave at the base of the cliff. The entrance was well hidden by the trees and bushes that grew there. He and his men used the hide-out for many years and hoarded their treasure there.

One day the huge rock overhanging the cave crumbled and fell.

It blocked the mouth of the cave and trapped the robbers inside. They never escaped and haunt it to this day.

On Ippikin's rock is the mark of the gold chain the knight used to wear. If anyone were bold enough to stand on the clifftop and shout out:

'Ippikin, Ippikin,
Keep away with your long chin!'

then the ghost of the robber will appear, wearing the gold chain round his neck, and throw the caller over the edge of the cliff to their death.

Wild Edric

The Old Men

In the hills around Minsterley, there are lead mines which have been worked since the days of the Romans. Deep underground, the rebel knight, Wild Edric, is imprisoned with his men. That was his punishment for making peace with William the Conqueror in the years after the Normans invaded England. He is only set free when the country is in danger and war is near. Then he and his men ride over the Stiperstones, to fight once more. He cannot die, they say, until all wrongs in the land have been put right, and England is free again.

In 1067, Edric joined forces with the Welsh kings to rebel against William, Duke of Normandy and King of England. They attacked the Norman stronghold of Hereford and carried off rich treasures. Two years later, almost every shire was in revolt against the Norman lords. For his part, Edric laid siege to Shrewsbury, but the rebellion failed, and Edric and his men were forced to make peace with William.

One day, in the middle of the last century, a young woman was out walking the hills with her father who was a miner. Suddenly she heard the blast of a hunting horn.

"It's the wild hunt!" her father told her. "Cover your face with your apron, and speak not a word or you will go mad!"

The girl did as she was told. Soon she felt the wind rushing by her and heard the thunder of hooves. Peeping over the edge of her apron, she saw the ghostly horsemen gallop by. At their head rode Wild Edric on a white horse. On his dark curly hair was a green cap with a feather. He wore a green tunic and cloak, and carried a horn and a short sword in his golden belt. Beside him rode the beautiful Lady Godda, his elfin wife, in a long green gown with a dagger in her belt. Her long golden hair hung loose to her waist, and in the white band round her forehead was an ornament of gold.

"Who are they?" asked the girl when the last of the riders had gone.

"We call them 'The Old Men'," said her father. "They have been imprisoned in the mines for many hundreds of years. Sometimes when we're working underground, we can hear them knocking. Wherever the noise comes from, we're sure to find the best lodes. But to see them riding out like this is a bad sign. It means the country is in danger."

The young woman was to remember the Wild Hunt and her father's warning, for some months later, the Crimean War broke out.

Edric and his Elf Bride

Edric Salvage held land at Weston-under-Redcastle and in the south of the shire. He used to go hunting wild boar and deer in the forests of Clun. One day he and his young page lost their way in the forest. They rode until nightfall, trying to find the path. At last, through the dark trees, they saw lights shining. Their horses were tired but they rode eagerly in the hope of a warm stable and shelter for the night. Soon they came to a large manor house. Edric had never noticed it in the forest before and he warned his page to be careful, for it might be the work of witchcraft. They were both so tired and hungry, they did not want to turn back.

"We'll go nearer and see just what kind of people live here," he said.

As they crept towards the windows, they could hear music playing. Peering in, they saw a room hung with rich tapestries and handsomely furnished. Edric stared in amazement. In the middle of the room a group of ladies in fine gowns danced gracefully in a circle. As they danced, they sang sweetly, but their language was none that Edric knew.

Edric watched for a while, uncertain whether to to in. He was more afraid than ever that this was the work of witchcraft. If he went inside, he feared he would come under some deadly spell. But as he watched, he noticed one of the young women, tall and

slender but more beautiful than the rest, and at once he fell in love. His fear of witchcraft vanished.

"Come on!" he told the page. "We must find a way in!" And he began to search around the walls of the house. At last he came to a door and forced his shoulder against it.

"Wait! It may be a trick!" the page warned him, but it was too late. Edric strode on down the hallway, searching for the dancers. The sound of the music drew him. He burst into the room where the women were dancing, and caught hold of the one he loved.

At first the women were so startled by Edric's sudden arrival that they went on dancing.

"I want you for my wife," Edric told the young woman and tried to pull her from the circle.

The dancing stopped. In fury, the women crowded round him, biting and scratching him. They pulled and tugged and tried to rescue their sister. Edric could feel her being dragged away from him.

"Help me!" he cried as his page rushed into the room after him. Between them, they managed to carry the young woman out of the house and rode off with her through the forest.

Edric found the way back to his castle at last, and ordered that the very best food and wine be brought for his bride. He told her he had fallen in love with her as he watched her dancing, and he begged her to forgive him for capturing her. The young woman said nothing.

Again Edric begged her to forgive him. He told her he would always love her and be kind to her. He told her she could have anything she wanted.

Still she said nothing. For three long days he told her of his love for her, and for three long days, she said nothing. Then at last she spoke.

"I will be your wife, Edric, and I will bring you happiness and good luck," she promised, "but you must never say one word against my sisters or my home, for on the day you do, you will lose both me and your good fortune. Then you will pine away and die."

Edric was overjoyed. He was determined never to speak of her sisters again. He set about arranging a magnificent wedding feast. Noblemen came from all over the land for the wedding and to admire Edric's beautiful bride. Even King William heard about Edric's marriage and asked to see her for himself. He didn't believe she could really be so beautiful, nor that she was of elvish blood. Edric travelled to William's court in London. He took his page with him to tell the King how they had first seen the woman dancing with her sisters. But the moment the King set eyes on the lady he had no need of any witness. He knew that all he had heard about her was true.

For some time Edric lived happily with his new wife. He was as kind to her as he had promised, and in return she gave him good health and good fortune as she had promised. Then, one evening, Edric came home from a hunting trip and could not find his lady anywhere in the castle. He was tired and ill-tempered after a long day's riding, and began to shout her name. At last she returned to him. Edric scowled at her.

"I suppose you've been seeing those sisters of yours!" he said angrily. Before he could say another word, she vanished.

Too late Edric remembered her warning before their wedding: 'Never say one word against my sisters...'

Long weeks he searched for her in the forests. He tried to find the house where he had first seen her, but he never saw her again. The years passed, and Edric pined away and died.

King Arthur and the Red Castle

The Red castle at Hawkstone takes its name from the red sandstone cliffs on which it is built. Early in the thirteenth century it was owned by Sir Henry de Audley, one of Fulk FitzWarin's enemies. At that time, the castle had four gateways and tall towers. Now only the ridges of its outer walls can be seen, and the ruined tower, cut into the rock, called 'The Giant's Well'.

Legends about the castle recall the days of King Arthur. Nearby, at Bury Walls, Roman coins and bricks have been found, and an old Roman road runs nearby. It is said that there was once an ancient city here, where King Arthur held his court.

In King Arthur's time, two giants owned the castle. They were called Tarquin and Tarquinus. The ruined tower is named the "Giant's Well" after them. Their brother, Sir Carados, was a fearsome fighter who had killed and imprisoned many knights in the castle. Sir Lancelot and Sir Tristam of the Round Table heard that he had captured their friend, Sir Gawain, and they rode to his rescue. When they caught up with the giant, they saw he carried Sir Gawain tied up and slung across his saddle. Sir Lancelot challenged Sir Carados to fight. For hours the two fought until at last, at the Killyards near Weston Church, Sir Lancelot killed the giant and set Sir Gawain free.

Another legend tells that two brothers, Sir Edward and Sir Hugh, held the castle. They had cheated a lady of her money and land,

41

and forced her to live on a rock ledge called "The Raven's Shelf". When King Arthur's knight, Sir Ewaine, came to fight at a tournament in the Marches, he heard about the Lady of the Rock and promised to help her.

He sent word to the two brothers, asking them to talk with him, but they came to meet him with one hundred of their men. The Lady would not let Sir Ewaine face them alone. Instead he called down to them, and challenged the brothers to fight.

"You will have to fight us both," the brothers told him. "And if we lose, we will give the Lady back her land."

Sir Ewaine accepted. The next day he rode out to fight them. For five hours they battled and Sir Ewaine was badly wounded, but he managed to kill Sir Edward. Then Sir Hugh gave in and agreed to return the lands he had taken, and he promised to go to King Arthur's court and make peace.

According to the Legend of Fulk FitzWarin, when King Arthur had lost his sense of chivalry, he came to stay at the chapel of St. Augustine near Whittington. There at last he found his courage and goodness again.

The Legend
of
Fulk Fitzwarin

"Out of the land of the White Plain will come a wolf with sharp teeth," said Merlin. "Its courage and strength will drive the leopard from the land."

So begins the Legend of Fulk FitzWarin, whose family crest was notched with silver like wolf's teeth. His old enemy, King John, had a coat of arms with leopards of beaten gold.

The Chess Game

The White Tower, which we now call Whittington, once belonged to the FitzWarin family, but they lost it in battle to the Prince of Wales who gave it to his cousin, Roger de Powis.

The young FitzWarin was named Fulk after his father and grandfather. He and his brothers were brought up with King Henry's sons. Fulk was well loved by all the princes except John. John had a reputation for being spiteful and envious - and a bad loser. One day, when the two boys were playing chess, John overturned the chessboard and hit Fulk. Fulk struck back. The prince fell over and hit his head. When John didn't move, Fulk was afraid he had killed him. He helped the boy to his feet, but John went at once to tell his father.

"You probably deserved it," King Henry said, and instead of being angry with Fulk, he punished John for telling tales. John could not forgive Fulk, and from that day on, he bore a grudge against him.

The White Tower

When King Henry died, Richard Coeur de Lion became King. He gave Fulk and his brothers fine armour and horses, and made them his knights. When Richard set sail for the Holy Land to fight in the Crusades, he made Fulk 'Lord of the Marches' to keep the border country safe from Welsh invaders until he returned.

But Richard died and John became King of England. He had not forgotten the grudge he bore Fulk. Nor had Fulk's enemies. The White Tower belonged to Moris de Powis and he wanted to make sure Fulk did not get it back. He sent King John a gift of a horse and a falcon and promised him £100 if he could keep the White Tower. The land was Fulk's by right, but the King was glad of the chance to spite him.

"The White Tower shall be yours to keep," he told Moris. "And I make you Lord of the Marches."
When Fulk and his brothers heard this, they went at once to the King and offered him £100, but King John would not change his mind. Fulk was angry.
"If you won't give me back my castle, I will not serve you!" he told the king, and walked out of his court.

King John sent his knights after him.
"Bring me back FitzWarin's head!" he told them. Fulk fought and killed many of the knights and escaped. The rest went back to the King empty-handed. King John was furious and swore revenge against the rebel knight.

King John's Merchants

Fulk did not wait for King John's knights to come after him. He left his castle at Alberbury and fled with his brothers to France. Then he heard that King John had taken more of his lands and given it to his friends.

"I can't let him get away with it!" Fulk thought. But he had no army to equal the King's. "But I can make life difficult for King John and his friends."

Secretly he returned to England and spied on Moris. But Moris was warned that Fulk was near. Carrying his shield of two golden boars, Moris set out with 500 footmen and knights. Fulk and his men rode out of the forests to do battle. Fulk wounded Moris in the shoulder, but as Moris fled back to his castle, he shot Fulk in the leg with an arrow. When King John heard of this, he offered a reward to anyone who could capture Fulk, dead or alive.

Fulk and his men lived in secret in Breidden forest. One day, some of King John's merchants rode by, bringing rich cloth, furs and treasures from abroad for the King. Fulk saw his chance to annoy the king and set upon the merchants. The merchants fought hard but they were soon overpowered.

"Who will bear this loss if I take the goods you carry?" Fulk asked them.

"As long as we fight to protect them and don't lose them by our cowardice, then King John will bear the loss," the merchants told him. So Fulk took all the goods they carried and dressed his men richly. Then he gave a feast for the merchants and sent them on their way.

"Give King John my best wishes," he told them, "And be sure to thank him for our fine new clothes!"

Of course this made the King all the more furious. At once he increased the reward for Fulk's life to £1,000.

The Crippled Monk

The King's men tracked Fulk south. They circled the forest where Fulk and his men were in hiding, and prepared a hunt. They set men in the fields to keep watch. If they saw Fulk or any of his men coming out of the forest, they were to blow their horns and give warning. But Fulk heard a bugle and realised danger was near. He and his men tried to escape, but each time they rode out of the forest, they saw the King's men waiting. At last they found a way out where only one bugler stood. Before he could sound the alarm, they killed him, and escaped to a nearby abbey where they took shelter.

Seeing the monks' habits gave Fulk an idea. He put on one of the gowns and taking a crutch, he limped out of the abbey. A group of knights rode up and asked him if he'd seen Fulk and his men. Fulk pretended to be angry.

"Indeed I have!" he told them. "They barged past me, knocking me over!" he said, and pointed them in the opposite direction to the abbey. The knights rode away, leaving Fulk and his men to make their escape.

The False Knight

Only those who supported King John had cause to fear Fulk.

He had many friends who would hide him, like the Scottish knight, Robert FitzSamson. But in the north there was a wicked knight, Piers de Bruvile, who disguised himself as Fulk and robbed and murdered in his name.

One day Fulk came to Robert's castle and saw there was a feast being held, but as he reached the hall he saw the masked knights of Piers and his robber band were seated round the tables. Robert and his household were tied up in a corner.

In fury, Fulk drew his sword. He strode down the hall and swore to kill anyone who moved.
"Tie up your men or I'll cut off your head!" he ordered. Piers did as he was told, but as soon as the robbers were tied up, Fulk had them killed and then cut off Piers' head too.

Robert and his family were freed, and they had a great feast of celebration.

The Minstrel

When Fulk returned to Alberbury Castle, he dared his friend John to go to Whittington and find out what his enemy, Moris, was up to. John could juggle and play music so he disguised himself as a minstrel. He ate a herb which made his face swell and discolour so that he would not be recognised. Dressed in poor clothes, he went to the castle. He told Moris he had come from Scotland and that Fulk was dead. At first Moris would not believe him.

"I swear it's true!" John said. "Everyone there says so," he told him, which was true since Piers had been using Fulk's name. Moris believed him then and gave John a silver cup for bringing him such good news. He also told John that he was riding to Shrewsbury next day.

Early next morning, Fulk lay in wait at Nesscliffe for Moris and his knights. Moris saw him at the roadside.

"Thieves!" he called them. "Your heads will be spiked and placed on the high tower of Shrewsbury Castle by evening!" At that, the two sides began to fight. Angry at how Moris had wronged him, Fulk fought hard and Moris and his knights were all killed.

The Flooded Ford

With Moris dead, Fulk feared the King's revenge. He fled to shelter with Llewellyn, Prince of Wales. They had been brought up together in King Henry's household and Llewellyn had married John's sister, Joan. Fulk made Llewellyn promise to defend him against King John. Only then did Fulk tell him that he had killed Moris, for Moris was Llewellyn's cousin. The prince was angry with him.

"But I promised to protect you," Llewellyn said, "And I will keep my word."

When King John learned that Fulk was staying with Llewellyn and his sister, he summoned all his earls, barons and knights to meet at Shrewsbury.

"I haven't been able to catch Fulk yet" he told them, "but I swear I shall take revenge against Llewellyn for sheltering him!"

Fulk promised to help defend Llewellyn against the king. He knew the country well. There was a narrow ford the King would have to cross. He set his men to dig a deep ditch and flood the land. Then he set up a barricade.

When the King came with his army, Fulk took some of his best knights and rode out to fight him. The King's men could not ride round and avoid them because the land was too marshy for their horses. They had to fight. But they were too many for Fulk. He and his men drew back behind the barricade and let the archers have their turn. Under a hail of arrows, the King turned tail and retreated to Shrewsbury.

The Ethiopian

After Moris's death, Prince Llewellyn gave Whittington Castle back to Fulk. But John Lestrange wanted the castle and complained to the King. King John sent Sir Henry de Audley to attack Whittington where Fulk was celebrating with the Welsh knights. The two sides met near Myddle. John Lestrange attacked Fulk but his lance shattered. Fulk's blow struck him through his helmet. Lestrange fell from his horse and in fury called all his men to attack Fulk. Two of Fulk's brothers were wounded. When Fulk saw this, he was maddened with anger. He spurred his horse into the midst of the fighting. But Fulk and his seven hundred knights were no match for Henry de Audley's thousands. Fulk was forced to retreat to Whittington. As they

51

rode away, Fulk's friend, Sir Audulf de Bracy, was knocked from his horse and Sir Henry took him prisoner.

Sir Henry handed his prisoner over to King John.

"Sir Audulf is a robber and a traitor! I'll have him drawn and hanged!" the King swore.

As soon as Fulk realised Sir Audulf was missing, he sent John de Rampaigne to search for him. John blacked his face and hands and put on rich clothes. With a small drum slung round his neck, he rode to Shrewsbury Castle, disguised as an Ethiopian minstrel. He told King John,
"Sire, you are the most renowned in Christendom," which pleased the King. King John did not hear him add in a whisper that he was the most renowned for doing evil!

John de Rampaigne's music pleased the Court. That evening, Sir Henry sent for him to play in his private chamber. As he drank more and more wine, Sir Henry boasted of their prisoner and told the guards to fetch him.

"One good night shall he have before he dies," he told John, for Sir Audulf was to be hanged the next day. John knew he had little time to save his friend. When Sir Audulf was brought into the chamber, John played a song he had once known and so Sir Audulf recognised him despite his disguise, and knew that help was at hand.

John served Sir Henry and his men to more wine. As he poured out their drinks, he slipped a sleeping potion into the wine. As soon as the men were asleep, John freed Sir Audulf. He set one of the King's fools between Sir Audulf's sleeping guards, then, tying the sheets and towels together, they climbed down from the tower and escaped.

Fulk and the King of France

In his anger at their escape, King John hatched a new plan to capture Fulk. He sent word to Prince Llewellyn that he would give him back all his lands in return for Fulk's body. Llewellyn's wife, Joan, found the message and warned Fulk. Fulk prepared to leave at once.

"I have to go away," he told Llewellyn, "for I can no longer trust you to keep your word to me."

"Haven't I promised to protect you?" Llewellyn said.
"Yes, but you didn't warn me about the King's offer to you - your land for my body. I think the temptation might be too much for you."

So Fulk and his knights sailed to France. They came upon King Philip of France and his knights jousting in the meadows, and joined in. Their courage and skill at jousting won the King's approval, and he invited them to stay with him.

For some time Fulk was happy, travelling the country from tournament to tournament. They were well-loved by the King and his people although Fulk had never told him his true name. Then King John heard that Fulk was in France. At once he wrote to King Philip and begged him to banish the traitor. King Philip swore that no-one called Fulk was at his court. When Fulk heard this, he went to the King and asked his permission to leave.

"Are you unhappy in my Court? Is there anything you need here?" the King asked him.

"No, Sire," Fulk told him. "Only I have heard news that makes it impossible for me to stay."

Then King Philip understood that he was really Fulk FitzWarin. He was impressed by Fulk's sense of honour.

"You are free to stay," he told him. "I will give you more lands and wealth here than you ever had in England."

But Fulk refused. "If I cannot have my rightful estates, then I don't deserve to be given any others."

A Wolf in Sheep's Clothing

For a year Fulk sailed round the English coast, attacking any of King John's ships he came across. One day he landed at a Scottish island to look for food. A shepherd took him and his men back to his cave to get supplies. The shepherd gave six loud blasts on his horn.

"It's to call my servants," he told Fulk.

But six tall ruffians came into the cave, and challenged Fulk and his men to play chess. Each of Fulk's men was beaten. Fulk did not trust the men and when it came to his turn, he refused to play. At that, the biggest of the ruffians seized him and told him he'd play or fight. Fulk sprang up and, drawing his sword, cut off

54

the man's head. His men killed the other ruffians. They went into a second chamber and saw an old woman. She snatched up a horn to summon help, but she could not make it sound. In the chamber beyond were seven young women, all richly dressed. They fell to their knees in fear and begged Fulk's mercy.

"I am the daughter of Aunflorreis, King of Orkney," said one of the women. "And these are my maids. We sailed from our castle with four knights but this woman's seven sons came and killed the knights and took us prisoner."

Fulk took the young women back to his ship with some of the treasure they found in the caves. The he gave a loud blast on the horn. From all over the island, thieves came running. Fulk and his men fought and killed them all. He set sail for Orkney and returned the princess and her maids to the King.

The Winged Dragon

Fulk sailed on north to Scandinavia, and further north still, until the sea froze and the cold grew unbearable. Then he turned back for England. But a storm blew up and for fifteen days the ship could make no headway. At last they came to an island and anchored there to find food. The castle and all the fields around were deserted.

"Who does this land belong to?" Fulk asked an old peasant.

"It belongs to the Duke of Carthage," the man said. "But we live in terror of a dragon. It's killed nearly every man and beast

55

around. One day it seized the princess from the top of the tower. It carried her off to its lair on the mountain in the sea, and ate her."

Fulk set sail for the mountain in the sea where the dragon lived.

"Let's turn back while we still can," the helmsman begged him. But Fulk refused.

"We have fair weather and can see nothing wrong. Are we to die of fear?"

Taking Audulf with him, Fulk climbed the mountain. The path was littered with swords and armour. At the top there was a tree and a spring of clear water, and nearby he saw a cave. Fulk drew his sword and went in. Inside the dark cave he heard someone crying. Then he saw a beautiful young woman.

"I am the daughter of the Duke of Carthage," she told him. "A dragon brought me here seven years ago, and here I have been his prisoner ever since. Everyone who comes here is killed and eaten by the dragon. You must go before it returns."

"Has the dragon harmed you?" Fulk asked her. She shook her head.

"But when he has feasted on human flesh, he makes me wash the blood from his face in that spring," she told him. "Then he rolls a stone across the cave so I cannot escape and lies down to sleep on his golden couch."

Fulk took her to Sir Audulf. Just then they saw the belch of flame and smoke as the dragon returned. Its great head and long claws hovered nearer. As it flew over them, its long tail lashed at Fulk's shield and broke it in two. Fulk managed to hit the dragon's head with his sword, but the blade could not pierce the dragon's horny skin.

Up into the sky the dragon soared once more, to begin its attack. This time Fulk stood behind the tree and waited till the dragon passed. Then he lunged out at the dragon's tail and cut it off. With a dreadful roar, the dragon turned and tried to snatch the woman and carry her off. Sir Audulf defended her, but the dragon seized him in his claws and almost crushed him. Fulk hit out once again and cut off one of the dragon's claws. Then with a fierce thrust, he stabbed the creature in the mouth and killed it.

The Charcoal Burner

Fulk returned to Carthage with the Duke's daughter and the dragon's treasure, and there they stayed until Sir Audulf's wounds had healed. When they reached England again, they heard that the King was at Windsor. Fulk and his men lay in wait in the woods for King John to go hunting. In the woods, Fulk met an old charcoal burner dressed all in black. Fulk bought his clothes from him and took his place at the fire.

Soon the king and three of his knights came by. Fulk knelt humbly in greeting. The King and his men made fun of him. Then they asked if he had seen any deer.

"Why, yes, Sire," Fulk told them. "A great beast with fine horns ran by. I'll show you where it went if you like."

The King and his men followed him to a thicket.
"Wait there," Fulk told them, "And I'll drive the beast out to you."

But as soon as he was out of sight, Fulk brought his men from hiding and they took King John and his knights prisoner.

"I should kill you as you threatened to kill me," Fulk told the King.

"Have mercy, I beg you!" pleaded King John.

"I shall spare you only if you promise to be my friend," said Fulk.

The King gladly gave his word and Fulk set him free.

Once safe back in his castle, however, King John told his knights he never meant to keep his promise to Fulk. He sent them out at once to capture Fulk. But John de Rampaigne had never trusted the King and followed him. He rode back to warn Fulk that the King was sending Sir James de Normandy and his army after him.

When Sir James reached the forest, Fulk was waiting. He took Sir James prisoner and changed horses. Then he gagged Sir James and swapped helmets with him and led his prisoner back to the King.

When King John saw them coming, he recognised the horses and harness and believed that Sir James really had taken Fulk prisoner. As a reward, he offered to kiss the knight he thought was Sir James. But Fulk, disguised by the helmet, couldn't risk being recognised.

"I've no time to dismount, Sire," he told the King. "I must ride back at once and capture the rest of Fulk's knights for you."

The King was so impressed, he gave Fulk his horse to speed him on his way.

King John then gave orders for his prisoner to be executed.

The French knight, Emery de Pin, asked for the job of hanging the man they thought was Fulk. As the prisoner's helmet was taken off at last, Emery recognised it was his own cousin, Sir James.

Outwitted once more by Fulk, King John was mad with rage. "I shall never take off my coat of mail until Fulk is captured!" he swore, and set off with his knights on Fulk's trail.

A Fight to the Death

When Fulk returned to his men in the forest, he found his brother, William, had been badly wounded in the battle.

"Ride on without me. You must escape," William told him, but Fulk did not want to leave him to the mercy of King John and his army.

The Earl of Chester, an old friend of Fulk's, was the first to reach the forest.

"Surrender," he begged Fulk. "The King's army is too many for you. If you fight you will surely all be killed. Surrender, and I promise to protect you against the King's temper."

But Fulk knew better than to trust the King. Instead he asked the Earl to have William properly buried, and after the battle, to bury him and his men. The Earl was saddened by this but gave his word.

"You must do your duty to the King," Fulk told him. "And forget the old friendship between us."

So the Earl sounded the attack and the battle began. One of the knights stabbed Fulk with his sword. Though badly wounded, Fulk managed to turn and stab the man through the shoulder. The sword pierced the man's heart and lungs and he fell dead from his horse. But Fulk was weak from loss of blood and fainted. His sword fell from his hand. His brother John saw this and jumped up behind him on the horse. Holding tightly to him, he escaped from the battlefield. The King's men chased after them but could not catch them. All night they rode and next morning reached the coast where their ship was waiting, and set sail for Spain.

The Earl lost many men in the fight. As he searched the woods after the battle, he found Fulk's brother, William, still alive. Keeping his promise to Fulk, he sent him to a nearby abbey to be looked after. But King John heard of this and was angry with him for hiding Fulk's brother from him. Instead he had William brought to Windsor and threw him into a dungeon.

The King's Champion

For six days they sailed and Fulk could not sleep. At last they reached a remote and rocky island. Fulk's brothers went ashore to try and find food on the barren island, leaving Fulk asleep at last. But while they were away, a storm blew up and the ship tore loose from its moorings.

When Fulk woke, he saw the stars above him. He called for
his brothers but no-one came. Then he realised what had
happened. He was alone, and his brothers were stranded on the
island. He wept and cursed his fate, but soon fell deep asleep
again.

The ship drifted to Tunis where the King of Barbary,
Messobryn, was taking counsel with his admirals and four other
kings. When he saw the ship sail into port, he sent his men to
bring Fulk to his court and made him welcome. Isorie, the King's
sister, and her maids tended Fulk's wounds. He did not tell them
his real name or how he came to be there. Instead he said he
had been stabbed by a rival who loved the same woman, and set
adrift. Isorie took pity on him.

Fulk asked her about the armies he saw near the city.

"It's all because of the Duke of Carthage's daughter, Ydoine,"
she explained. "She was captured by a dragon and rescued by a
brave knight called Fulk FitzWarin.

"Indeed?" said Fulk, trying to sound surprised.

"After the Duke died, she became duchess and inherited his
lands. My brother, the King, asked her to marry him but she
refused. That hurt his pride so he sent his armies to burn down
her cities. She fled abroad to get help and now she's returned
with a great army at our borders. She's sent my brother a chal-
lenge. He must send his best knight to fight her champion. If her
knight loses, she promises to return in peace to her own country.
If my brother loses, he must repair all the damage he did." Isorie
looked at Fulk. "Will you fight on my brother's side?"

"Me? Fight for a Saracen against a Christian? I cannot," Fulk told her. "Unless your brother becomes a Christian, of course. Then I will do all I can to persuade the Duchess to marry him."

When the King heard what Fulk had said, he promised to become a Christian.

"I'll do anything to win the woman I love," he said.

"Then I will be your champion and fight for you," Fulk answered.

On the day of the battle, Fulk put on his armour and rode out to face the Duchess's champion. The two knights spurred their horses forward, and struck at each other. Their lances splintered. Then they drew their swords and fought on foot.

"Pagan!" the Duchess's knight cursed Fulk.

All day they fought but they were so evenly matched that neither seemed near to winning.

"Who are you and where are you from?" asked the Duchess's knight.

"Who are you?" Fulk countered.

"I am called Philip the Red," said the knight.

At that, Fulk gave a cry of joy.

"Then you are my brother! I thought you were dead by now! How did you escape from the island?"

"The Duchess rescued us," Philip told him. "Six long months we'd been there, with nothing to eat but our horses. When she asked us to fight on her behalf, we were glad to!"

"Then we must stop the fighting now," said Fulk.

Philip went back to the Duchess and told him who his opponent was. Fulk persuaded the King and his household to become Christian. Then the Duchess agreed to marry the King. They rewarded Fulk richly for his help in bringing peace to their countries.

The Rescue

Fulk and his men returned secretly to England. John de Rampaigne dressed as a Greek merchant and went to find out where the King was and if their brother, William, was still alive. Thanks to his rich presents, John was welcomed by the Mayor of London and was invited to dine with King John. He told the King of all the riches on his ship, and King John gave him his personal surety for the ship to come into port. As they dined, a poorly dressed knight was brought in. John recognised him as Fulk's brother, William FitzWarin. He returned to Fulk and told him his brother was still alive, but was King John's prisoner.

Fulk sailed his ship into the port of London. John took a fine horse as a gift for the King and many other gifts for the courtiers so that they could go where they pleased. The men armed themselves and put on merchants' robes. Then they set out from the ship for Westminster. There they saw William being taken back to prison. Quickly they overpowered the guards before the alarm could be raised, and took William back to the ship and escaped to France.

Peace

On Fulk's return to England, he learned that John was hunting in the New Forest. He came upon the King chasing a wild boar, and captured him and six of his knights. They took them all back to the ship. Then Fulk and King John talked long together until at last the old grievances between them were settled. The King agreed to be Fulk's friend once more, and to give him back all his lands. This time when Fulk set him free, he kept the six knights as hostages, to make sure the King kept his word.

When King John returned to Westminster, he summoned his earls and barons and clergy.

"I have freely granted my goodwill to Fulk FitzWarin and his family," he announced.

Then Fulk and his men dressed in their finest clothes. They rode through London and came to kneel before King John and swore their loyalty to him. The King welcomed them and there they stayed at his court for a month. At last Fulk returned to Whittington. He rewarded his men with horses and land, and settled down to live in peace with his family. As the years passed, he felt ashamed of the harm he had caused and the many men he had killed. He decided to build an abbey near his castle at Alberbury, beside the River Severn.

One night as he lay in bed thinking of his past misdeeds, a brilliant light filled the room. A voice boomed out:

"Knight, God has granted you your penance, which is worth more on earth than in heaven!"

The noise woke his wife and she covered her face in fear of the bright light. When the light faded, Fulk was blind for the rest of his life. He kept his promise. He built the abbey at Alberbury and led a good and generous life. He had the road altered so that it ran through his manor.

"No stranger will pass my house without food or lodging," he ordered. After his death, he was buried with his wife near the altar in the abbey he had founded.

Though the tales of his adventures may not all be true, it is certain that Fulk FitzWarin rebelled against the King in the year 1201 over the loss of his castle at Whittington. For two years he and many of his family lived as outlaws. He was pardoned, but rebelled against the King again at Easter 1215. Not until after King John's death was he pardoned again and given back his lands.

Even after that, Fulk FitzWarin was known to be a dangerous Marcher Lord and not to be trusted to be loyal to the King. In 1222, the King heard that Fulk was strengthening Whittington Castle. He asked the Earl of Chester to visit the castle and make sure Fulk wasn't making it stronger than need be just to keep out the Welsh.

It is likely that Fulk was blind during the last years of his life because his son was managing his estate for him.

The ruins of Whittington and Alberbury Castles can still be seen. As for the Abbey, little trace now remains. Originally it was known as the Black Abbey after the colour of the monks' habits. Over the years, its name changed to the White Abbey because of the white sandstone used to build it. Some of the old abbey now forms part of White Abbey Farm.